Andrew

Trademark of Random House, Inc., William Collins Sons & Co. Ltd., Authorised User

1 2 3 4 5 6 7 8 9 10

ISBN 0 00 171284 5 (paperback)

ISBN 0 00 171225 X (hardback)

© 1978 by Stanley and Janice Berenstain
A Bright and Early Book for Beginning Beginners
Published by arrangement with Random House, Inc. New York, New York
First published in Great Britain 1979

Printed & bound in Hong Kong

THE BERENSTAIN BEARS AND THE SPOOKY OLD TREE

Stan and Jan Berenstain

COLLINS

Three little bears.

One with a light.
One with a stick.
One with a rope.

A spooky old tree.

Do they dare go into
that spooky old tree?

Yes.
They dare.

Three little bears...
One with a light.
One with a stick.
One with a rope.

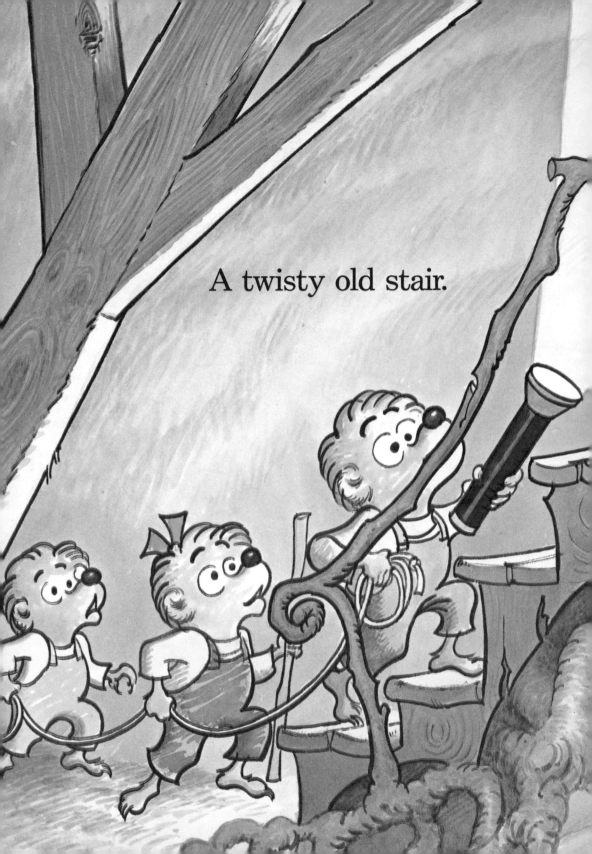

A twisty old stair.

Do they dare go up
that twisty old stair?

Yes.
They dare.

Three little bears.
One with a light.
One with a stick.
And <u>one</u> with the shivers.

A giant key.

A moving wall.

Will the three little bears
go through that wall?
Do they dare go into
that spooky old hall?

Three little bears.
One with a light.
And <u>two</u> with the shivers.

Great Sleeping Bear.

Do they dare go over
Great Sleeping Bear?

Do they dare?
Well...

They came into the tree.

They climbed the stair.

They went through the wall...

and into the hall.

So of course they went over
Great Sleeping Bear!

Three little bears...
without a light,
without a stick,
without a rope.
And <u>all</u> with the shivers!

How will they ever
get out of there?

Three little bears
running fast.

Home again.
Safe at last.